THE BR

By Anna Katharine Green (Mrs. Charles Rohlfs)

I. THE FASCINATING UNKNOWN.

HER room was on the ground floor of the house we mutually inhabited, and mine directly above it, so that my opportunities for seeing her were limited to short glimpses of her auburn head as she leaned out of the window to close her shutters at night or open them in the morning. Yet our chance encounter in the hall or on the walk in front, had made so deep an impression upon my sensibilities that I was never without the vision of her pale face set off by the aureole of reddish brown hair, which, since my first meeting with her, had become for me the symbol of everything beautiful, incomprehensible and strange.

For my fellow-lodger was a mystery.

I am a busy man now, but just at the time of which I speak, I had leisure in abundance.

I was sharing with many others the unrest of the perilous days subsequent to the raid of John Brown at Harper's Ferry. Abraham Lincoln had been elected President. Baltimore, where the incidents I am relating transpired, had become the headquarters of men who secretly leagued themselves in antagonism to the North. Men and women who felt that their Northern brethren had grievously wronged them planned to undermine the stability of the government. The schemes at this time were gigantic in their conception and far-reaching in their scope and endless ramifications.

Naturally under these conditions, a consciousness of ever-present danger haunted every thinking mind. The candor of the outspoken was regarded with doubt, and the reticence of the more cautious, with distrust. It was a trying time for sensitive, impressionable natures with nothing to do. Perhaps all this may account for the persistency with which I sat in my open window. I was thus sitting one night—a memorable one to me—when I heard a sharp exclamation from below, in a voice I had long listened for.

Any utterance from those lips would have attracted my attention; but, filled as this was with marked, if not extraordinary, emotion, I could not fail to be roused to a corresponding degree of curiosity and interest.

Thrusting out my head, I cast a rapid glance downward. A shutter swinging in the wind, and the escaping figure of a man hurrying round the corner of the street, were all that rewarded my scrutiny; though, from the stream of light issuing from the casement beneath, I perceived that her window, like my own, was wide open.

As I continued to watch this light, I saw her thrust out her head with an eagerness indicative of great excitement. Peering to right and left, she murmured some suppressed words mixed with gasps of such strong feeling that I involuntarily called out:

"Excuse me, madam, have you been frightened in any way by the man I saw running away from here a moment ago?"

She gave a great start and glanced up. I see her face yet—beautiful, wonderful; so beautiful and so wonderful I have never been able to forget it. Meeting my eye, she faltered out:

"Did you see a man running away from here? Oh, sir, if I might have a word with you!"

I came near leaping directly to the pavement in my ardor and anxiety to oblige her, but, remembering before it was too late that she was neither a Juliet nor I a Romeo, I merely answered that I would be with her in a moment and betook myself below by the less direct but safer means of the staircase.

It was a short one and I was but a moment in descending, but that moment was long enough for my heart to acquire a most uncomfortable throb, and it was with anything but an air of quiet self-possession that I approached the threshold I had never before dared to cross even in fancy.

The door was open and I caught one glimpse of her figure before she was aware of my presence. She was contemplating her right hand with a look of terror, which, added to her striking personality, made her seem at the instant a creature of alarming characteristics fully as capable of awakening awe as devotion.

I may have given some token of the agitation her appearance awakened, for she turned towards me with sudden vehemence.

"Oh!" she cried, with a welcoming gesture; "you are the gentleman from up-stairs who saw a man running away from here a moment ago. Would you know that man if you saw him again?"

"I am afraid not," I replied. "He was only a flying figure in my eyes."

"Oh!" she moaned, bringing her hands together in dismay. But, immediately straightening herself, she met my regard with one as direct as my own. "I need a friend," she said, "and I am surrounded by strangers."

I made a move towards her; I did not feel myself a stranger. But how was I to make her realize the fact?

"If there is anything I can do," I suggested.

Her steady regard became searching.

"I have noticed you before to-night," she declared, with a directness devoid of every vestige of coquetry. "You seem to have qualities that may be trusted. But the man capable of helping me needs the strongest motives that influence humanity: courage, devotion, discretion, and a total forgetfulness of self. Such qualifications cannot be looked for in a stranger."

As if with these words she dismissed me from her thoughts, she turned her back upon me. Then, as if recollecting the courtesy due even to strangers, she cast me an apologetic glance over her shoulder and hurriedly added:

"I am bewildered by my loss. Leave me to the torment of my thoughts. You can do nothing for me."

Had there been the least evidence of falsity in her tone or the slightest striving after effect in her look or bearing, I would have taken her at her word and left her then and there. But the candor of the woman and the reality of her emotion were not to be questioned, and moved by an impulse as irresistible as it was foolhardy, I cried with the impetuosity of my twenty-one years:

"I am ready to risk my life for you. Why, I do not know and do not care to ask. I only know you could have found no other man so willing to do your bidding."

A smile, in which surprise was tempered by a feeling almost tender, crossed her lips and immediately vanished. She shook her head as if in deprecation of the passion my words evinced, and was about to dismiss me, when she suddenly changed her mind and seized upon the aid I had offered, with a fervor that roused my sense of chivalry and deepened what might have been but a passing fancy into an active and all-engrossing passion.

"I can read faces," said she, "and I have read yours. You will do for me what I cannot do for myself, but——Have you a mother living?"

I answered no; that I was very nearly without relatives or ties.

"I am glad," she said, half to herself. Then with a last searching look, "Have you not even a sweetheart?"

I must have reddened painfully, for she drew back with a hesitating and troubled air; but the vigorous protest I hastened to make seemed to reassure her, for the next word she uttered was one of confidence.

"I have lost a ring." She spoke in a low but hurried tone. "It was snatched from my finger as I reached out my hand to close my shutters. Some one must have been lying in wait; some one who knows my habits and the hour at which I close my window for the night. The loss I have sustained is greater than you can conceive. It means more, much more, than appears. To the man who will bring me back that ring direct from the hand that stole it, I would devote the gratitude of a lifetime. Are you willing to make the endeavor? It is a task I cannot give to the police."

This request, so different from any I had expected, checked my enthusiasm in proportion as it awoke a senseless jealousy.

"Yet it seems directly in their line," I suggested, seeing nothing but humiliation before me if I attempted the recovery of a simple love-token.

"I know that it must seem so to you," she admitted, reading my thoughts and answering them with skilful indirectness. "But what policeman would undertake a difficult and minute search for an article whose intrinsic value would not reach five dollars?"

"Then it is only a memento," I stammered, with very evident feeling.

"Only a memento," she repeated; "but not of love. Worthless as it is in itself, it would buy everything I possess, and almost my soul to-night. I can explain no further. Will you attempt its recovery?"

Restored to myself by her frank admission that it was no lover's keepsake I was urged to recapture and return, I allowed the powerful individuality of this woman to have its full effect upon me. Taking in with one glance her beauty, the impassioned fervor of her nature, and the subtle charm of a spirit she now allowed to work its full spell upon me, I threw every practical consideration to the winds, and impetuously replied:

"I will endeavor to regain this ring for you. Tell me where to go, and whom to attack, and if human wit and strength can compass it, you shall have the jewel back before morn-ing.

"Oh!" she protested, "I see that you anticipate a task of small difficulty. You cannot recover this particular ring so easily as that. In the first place, I do not in the least know who took it; I only know its destination. Alas! if it is allowed to reach that destination, I am bereft of hope."

"No love token," I murmured, "and yet your whole peace depends on its recovery."

"More than my peace," she answered; and with a quick movement she closed the door which I had left open behind me. As its sharp bang rang through the room, I realized into what a pitfall I had stumbled. Only a political intrigue of the most desperate character could account for the words I had heard and the actions to which I had been a witness. But I was in no mood to recoil even from such dangers as these, and so my look showed her as she leaned toward me with the words:

"Listen! I am burdened with a secret. I am in this house, in this city, for a purpose. The secret is not my own and I cannot part with it; neither is my purpose communicable. You therefore will be obliged to deal with the greatest dangers blindfold. One encouragement only I can give you. You will work for good ends. You are pitted against wrong, not right, and if you succumb, it will be in a cause you yourself would call noble. Do I make myself understood, Mr.—Mr. ———"

"Abbott," I put in, with a bow.

She took the bow for an affirmative, as indeed I meant she should. "You do not recoil," she murmured, "not even when I say that you must take no third party into your confidence, no matter to what extremity you are brought."

"I would not be the man I think I am, if I recoiled," I said, smiling.

She waved her hand with almost a stern air.

"Swear!" she commanded; "swear that, from the moment you leave this door till you return to it, you will breathe no word concerning me, your errand, or even the oath I am now exacting from you."

"Ah!" thought I to myself, "this is serious." But I took the oath under the spell of the most forceful personality I had ever met, and did not regret it—then.

"Now let us waste no more time," said she.

"In the large building on ———— Street there is an office with the name of Dr. Merriam on the door. See! I have written it on this card, so that there may be no mistake about it. That office is open to patients from ten in the morning until twelve at noon. During these hours any one can enter there; but to awaken no distrust, he should have some ailment. Have you not some slight disorder concerning which you might consult a physician?"

"I doubt it," said I; "but I might manufacture one."

"That would not do with Dr. Merriam. He is a skilful man; he would see through any imposture."

"I have a sick friend," I ruminated. "And by the way, his case is obscure and curious. I could interest any doctor in it in five minutes."

"That is good; consult him in regard to your friend; meantime—while you are waiting for the interview, I mean—take notice of a large box you will find placed on a side-table. Do not seem to fix your attention on it, but never let it be really out of your sight from the moment the door is unlocked at ten till you are forced by the doctor's importunity to leave the room at twelve. If you are alone there for one minute (and you will be allowed to remain there alone if you show no haste to consult the doctor) unlock that box—here is the key—and look carefully inside. No one will interfere and no one will criticize you; there is more than one person who has access to that box."

"But—" I put in.

"You will discover there," she whispered, "a hand of bronze lying on an enamelled cushion. On the fingers of this hand there should be, and doubtless are, rings of forged steel of peculiar workmanship. If there is one on the middle finger, my cause is lost, and I can only await the end." Her cheek paled. "But if there is not, you may be sure that an attempt will be made by some one to-morrow—I do not know whom—to put one there before the office closes at noon. The ring will be mine—the one stolen from my hand just now—and it will be your business to prevent the box being opened for this purpose, by any means short of public interference involving arrest and investigation; for this, too, would be fatal. The delay of a day may be of incalculable service to me. It would give me time to think, if not to act. Does the undertaking seem a hopeless one? Am I asking too much of your inexperience?"

"It does not seem a hopeful one," I admitted; "but I am willing to undertake the adventure. What are its dangers? And why, if I see the ring on the finger you speak of, cannot I take it off and bring it back to you?"

"Because," said she, answering the last question first, "the ring becomes a part of the mechanism the moment it is thrust over the last joint. You could not draw it off. As for the dangers I allude to, they are of a hidden character, and part of the secret I mentioned. If, however, you exercise your wit, your courage, and a proper amount of strategy, you may escape. Interference must be proved against you. That rule, at least, has been held inviolate."

Aghast at the mysterious perils she thus indicated in the path toward which she was urging me, I for one instant felt an impulse to retreat. But adventure of any kind has its allurements for an unoccupied youth of twenty-one, and when seasoned, as this was, by a romantic, if unreasonable, passion, proved altogether too irresistible for me to give it up. Laughing outright in my endeavor to throw off the surplus of my excitement, I drew myself up and uttered some fiery phrase of courage, which I doubt if she even heard. Then I said some word about the doctor, which she at once caught up.

"The doctor," said she, "may know, and may not know, the mysteries of that box. I would advise you to treat him solely as a doctor. He who uses the key you now hold in your hand cannot be too wary; by which I mean too careful or too silent. Oh, that I dared to go there myself! But my agitation would betray me. Besides, my person is known, or this ring would never have been taken from me.

"I will be your deputy," I assured her. "Have you any further instructions?"

"No," said she; "instructions are useless in an affair of this kind. Your actions must be determined by the exigencies of the moment. Meantime, my every thought will be yours. Good-night, sir; pray God, it may not be good-by."

"One moment," I said, as I arose to go. "Have you any objection to telling me your name?"

"I am Miss Calhoun," she said, with a graceful bow.

This was the beginning of my formidable adventure with the bronze hand.

II. THE QUAKER-LIKE GIRL, THE PALE GIRL, AND THE MAN WITH A BRISTLING MUSTACHE.

THE building mentioned by my new-found friend was well known to me. It was one of the kind in which every other office is unoccupied the year round. Such tenants as gave it the little air of usefulness it possessed were of the bad-pay kind. They gave little concern to their own affairs and less to those of their neighbors. The public avoided the building, and the tenants did nothing to encourage a change. In a populous city, on the corner made by frequented streets, it stood as much alone and neglected as if it were a ruin. Old or young eyes may have looked through its begrimed windows into the busy thoroughfare beneath, but none in the street ever honored the old place with a glance or thought. No one even wasted contempt upon its smoky walls, and few disturbed the accumulated dust upon the stairs or in the dimly-lighted hallways.

Had a place been sought for wherein the utmost secrecy might be observed, surely this was that place. As I neared the door upon which I read the doctor's name, I found myself treading on tip-toe, so impressed had I become by a sense of caution, if not of dread.

I had made every effort to be on hand at precisely ten o'clock, and felt so sure that I had been the first to arrive that I reached out to the door-knob with every expectation of entering, unseen by any one, and possibly unheard. To my dismay, the first twist I gave it resulted in a rusty shriek that set my teeth on edge, and echoed down the gloomy hall. With my flesh creeping, I opened the door and passed into the doctor's outer room.

It was far from being empty. Seated in chairs ranged along two sides of the room, I saw a dozen or more persons, male and female.

All wore the preoccupied air that patients are apt to assume while awaiting their turn to be called by the doctor. One amongst the number made an effort at indifference by drawing out and pushing back a nail in the flooring with the sole of her pretty shoe. It may have been intended for coquetry, and at another time might have bewitched me; now it seemed strangely out of place. The man who was to all appearance counting the flies in the web of an industrious spider was more in keeping with the place, my feelings, and the atmosphere of despondency that the room gave out.

As I had no doubt that the ring I was seeking was in the possession of some one of these persons, I gave each as minute an examination as was possible under the circumstances. Only two amongst them appeared open to suspicion. Of these, one was a young man whose naturally fine features would have prepossessed him in my favor had it not been for the peculiar alertness of his bright blue eye, which flashed incessantly in every direction till each and all of us seemed to partake of his restlessness and anxiety. Why was he not depressed? The other was the girl, or, rather, the young lady to whose pretty foot I have referred. If she was at all conspicuous, it was owing to the contrast between her beautiful face and the Quaker-like simplicity of her dress. She was restless also; her foot had ceased its action, but her hand moved constantly. Now it clutched its fellow in her lap, and now it ran in an oft-repeated action, seemingly beyond her control, up and down and round and round a plain but expensive leather bag she wore at her side. "She carries the ring," thought I, sitting down in the chair next her.

Meantime, I had not been oblivious of the box. It stood upon a plain oak table directly opposite the door by which I had come in. It was about a foot square, and was the only object in the room at all ornamental. Indeed, there was but little else for the eye to rest on, consequently most of us looked that way, though I noticed that but few seemed to take any real interest in that or anything else within sight. This was encouraging, and I was on the point of transferring my entire attention to the two persons I have named, when one of them, the nearest, rose hurriedly and went out.

This was an unexpected move on her part, and I did not know what to make of it. Had I annoyed her by my scrutiny, or had she divined my errand? In my doubt, I consulted the face of the man I secretly thought to be her accomplice. It was non-committal, and, in my doubt as to the meaning of all this, I allowed myself to become interested in a pale young woman who had been sitting on the other side of the lady who had just left. She was evidently a patient who stood in great need of assistance. Her head hung feebly forward, and her whole figure looked ready to drop. Yet when a minute later the door of the inner office opened, and the doctor appeared on the sill in an expectant attitude, she made no attempt to rise, but pushed forward another woman who seemed less indisposed than herself. I had to compel myself to think of all I saw as being real and within my experience.

Surprised by this action on the part of one so ill, I watched the pale girl for an instant, and almost forgot my mission in the compassion aroused by her sickly appearance. But soon that mission and my motive for being in this place were somewhat vividly recalled to me by an unexpected action on this very young woman's part. With the sudden movement of an acutely suffering person, she bounded from her seat and crossed the floor to where the box stood, gasping for breath, and almost falling against the table when she reached it.

A grunt from the good-looking young man followed; but neither he nor the middle-aged female with a pitiful skin disease, who had been sitting near her, offered to go to her assistance, though the latter looked as if she would like to. I was the only one to rise. The truth is, I could see no one touch the box without having something more than my curiosity awakened. Approaching her respectfully, and with as complete a dissimulation of my real feelings as possible, I ventured to say:

"You are very ill, miss. Shall I summon the doctor?"

She was clutching the side of the table for support, and her head, drooping helplessly over the box, was swaying from side to side as she rocked to and fro in her pain.

"Thank you!" she gasped, without turning, "I will wait. I would rather wait."

At that moment the doctor's door opened again.

"There he is now," said I.

"I will wait," she insisted. "Let the others take their turn."

Satisfied now that something besides pain caused her interest in the box, I drew back, asking myself whether she had been in possession of the ring from the beginning, or whether it had been passed to her by her restless neighbor. Meanwhile, another patient had disappeared into the adjoining room.

A few minutes passed. The man with the restless eye began to fidget. Could it be that she was simply guarding the box, and that he was the one who wished to open it? As the doubt struck me, I surveyed her more attentively. She was certainly doing something besides supporting herself with that sly right hand of hers. Yes, that was a click I heard. She was fitting a key into the lock. Startled, but determined not to betray myself, I assumed an air of great patience, and, taking a memorandum book from my pocket, began to write in it. Meantime, the doctor had disposed of his second patient and had beckoned to a third. To my astonishment, my friend with the nervous manner responded, thus acquitting himself in my eyes from any interest in the box.

The interview he had with the doctor lasted some time; meantime, the young woman in the window remained more or less motionless. When the fourth person left the room, she turned and cast a quick glance at myself and the other person present.

I knew what it meant. She was anxious to be left alone in order to lift that mysterious lid. She was no more ill than I was.

There was even a dash of color in her cheeks, and the trembling she indulged in was caused by great excitement and suspense, and not by pain.

Compassion at once gave way to anger, and I inwardly resolved not to spare her if we came into conflict over the box.

My companion was an old and non-observant man, who had come in after the rest of us. When the doctor again appeared, I motioned to this old man to follow him, which he very gladly did, leaving me alone with the pale girl. At once I got up, showing my fatigue and slightly yawning.

"This is very tedious," I muttered aloud, and stepped idly towards the door leading into the hall.

The girl at the box could not restrain her impatience. She cast me another short glance. I affected not to see it; took out my watch, consulted it, put it back quickly and slipped out into the hall. As I closed the door behind me, I heard a slight creak. Instantly I was back again, and with so sudden a movement that I surprised her, with her face bent over the open box.

"Oh, my poor young lady," I exclaimed, springing towards her with every appearance of great concern. "You do not look able to stand. Lean on me if you feel faint, and I will help you to a seat."

She turned upon me in a fury, but, meeting my eye, assumed an air of composure, which did not impose upon me in the least, or prevent me from pressing close to her side and taking one look into the box, which she had evidently not had sufficient self-possession to close.

The sight which met my eye was not unexpected, yet was no less interesting on that account. A hand—the hand—curiously made of bronze, and of exquisite proportions, lay on its enamelled cushion, with rings on all of its fingers save one. That one I was delighted to see was the middle one, proof positive that the mischief contemplated by Miss Calhoun had not yet been accomplished.

Restored to complete self-possession by this discovery, I examined the box and its contents with an air of polite curiosity. I surprised myself by my self-possession and bonhomie.

"What an odd thing to find in a physician's office!" I exclaimed. "Beautiful, is it not? An unusual work of art; but there is nothing in it to alarm you. You shouldn't allow yourself to be frightened at such a thing as that." And with a quick action, she was wholly powerless to prevent, I shut down the lid, which closed with a snap.

Startled and greatly discomposed, she drew back, hastily thrusting her hand behind her.

"You are very officious," she began, but, seeing nothing but good nature in the smile with which I regarded her, she faltered irresolutely, and finally took refuge again in her former trick of invalidism. Breaking out into low moanings, she fell back upon the nearest chair, from which she immediately started again with the quick cry, "Oh, how I suffer! I am not well enough to be out alone." And turning with a celerity that belied her words, she fled into the hall, shutting the door violently behind her.

Astonished at the completeness of my victory, I spent the first moments of triumph in trying to lift the lid of the box. But it was securely locked. I was just debating whether I could now venture to return to my seat, when the hall door reopened and a gentleman entered.

He was short, sturdy and had a bristling black mustache. I needed to look at him but once to be certain he was interested both in the box and me, and, while I gave no evidence of my discovery, I prepared myself for an adventure of a much more serious nature than that which had just occupied me.

Modeling my behavior upon that of the young girl whose place I had usurped, I placed my elbow on the box and looked out of the window. As I did so I heard a shuffling in the adjoining room, and knew that in another moment the doctor would again appear at the door to announce that he was ready for another patient. How could I evade the summons? The man behind me was a determined one. He was there for the purpose of opening the box, and would not be likely to leave the room while I remained in it. How, then, could I comply with the requirements of the situation and yet prevent this new-comer from lifting the lid in my absence? I knew of but one way—a way which had suggested itself to me during the long watches of the previous night, and which I had come prepared to carry out.

Taking advantage of my proximity to the box, I inserted in the keyhole a small morsel of wax which for some minutes past I had been warming in my hand. This done, I laid my hat down on the lid, noting with great exactness as I did so just where its rim lay in reference to the various squares and scrolls with which the top was ornamented. By this means I felt that I might know if the hat were moved in my absence. The doctor having showed himself by this time, I followed him into his office with a calmness born of the most complete confidence in the strategy I had employed.

Dr. Merriam, whom I have purposely refrained from describing until now, was a tall, well-made man, with a bald head and a pleasant eye, but careless in his attire and bearing. As I met that eye and responded to his good-natured greeting, I inwardly decided that his interest in the box was much less than his guardianship of it would seem to betoken. And when I addressed him and entered upon the subject of my friend's complaint, I soon saw by the depth of his professional interest that whatever connection he might have with the box, neither that nor any other topic whatever could for a moment vie with his delight in a new and strange case like that of my poor friend. I consequently entered into the medical details demanded of me with a free mind and succeeded in getting some very valuable advice, for which I was of course truly grateful.

As soon as this was accomplished I took my leave, but not by the usual door of egress. Saying that I had left my hat in the ante-room, I bowed my acknowledgments to the doctor and returned the way I came. But not without meeting with a surprise. There was still but one person in the room with the box, but that person was not the man with the bristling mustache and determined eye whom I had expected to find there. It was the pretty, Quaker-like girl who had formerly aroused my suspicions; and though she sat far from the box, a moment's glance at her flushed face and trembling hands assured me she had but that moment left it.

Going at once to the box, I saw that my hat had been moved. But more significant still was the hairpin lying on the floor at my feet, with a morsel of wax sticking to one of its points. This was conclusive. The man had discovered why his key would not work, and had called to his aid the young lady, who had evidently been waiting in the hall outside.

She had tried to pick out the wax—a task in which I had happily interrupted her.

Proud of the success of my device, and satisfied that the danger was over for that day (it being well on to twelve o'clock), I said a few words more to the doctor, who had followed me into the room, and then prepared to take my departure. But the young lady was more agile than I. Saying something about a very pressing engagement which would not allow her to consult the doctor that day, she hurried ahead of me and ran quickly down the long hall. The doctor looked astonished, but dismissed the matter with a shrug; while, with the greatest desire to follow her, I stood hesitating on the threshold, when my eye fell on a small object lying under the chair on which she had been sitting. It was the little leathern bag I had seen hanging at her side.

Catching it up, I explained that I would run after the young lady and restore it; and glad of an excuse which would enable me to follow her through the streets without risking the suspicion of impropriety, I hastened down the stairs and happily succeeded in reaching the pavement before her skirts whisked round the corner. I was therefore but a few paces behind her, which distance I took good care to preserve.

III. MADAME.

My motive in following this young girl was not so much to restore her property, as to see where her engagement was taking her. I felt confident that none of the three persons who had shown interest in the box was the prime mover in an affair so important; and it was necessary above all things to find out who the prime mover was. So I followed the girl.

She led me into a doubtful quarter of the town. As the crowd between us diminished and we reached a point where we were the only pedestrians on the block we were then traversing, I grew anxious lest she should turn and see me before arriving at her destination. But she evidently was without suspicion, for she passed without any hesitation up a certain stoop in the middle of this long block and entered an open door on which a brass plate was to be seen, inscribed with this one word in large black letters:

"MADAME."

This was odd; and as I had no inclination to encounter any "madame" without some hint as to her character and business, I looked about me for some one able and willing to give me the necessary information. An upholsterer's shop in an opposite basement seemed to offer me the opportunity I wanted. Crossing the street, I saluted the honest-looking man I met in the doorway, and pointing out madame's house, asked what was done over there.

He answered with a smile.

"Go and see," he said; "the door's open. Oh, they don't charge anything," he made haste to protest, misunderstanding, no doubt, my air of hesitation. "I was in there once myself. They all sit round and she talks; that is, if she feels like it. It is all nonsense, you know, sir; no good in it."

"But is there any harm?" I asked. "Is the place reputable and safe?"

"Oh, safe enough; I never heard of anything going wrong there. Why, ladies go there; real ladies; veiled, of course. I have seen two carriages at a time standing in front of that door. Fools, to be sure, sir; but honest enough, I suppose."

I needed no further encouragement. Recrossing the street, I entered the house which stood so invitingly open, and found myself almost immediately in a large hall, from which I was ushered by a silent negress into a long room with so dim and mysterious an interior that I felt like a man suddenly transported from the bustle of the out-door world into the mystic recesses of some Eastern temple.

The causes of this effect were simple, A dim light suggesting worship; the faint scent of slowly burning incense; women and men sitting on low benches about the walls. In the center, on a kind of raised dais, backed by a drapery of black velvet, a woman was seated, in the semblance of a Hindoo god, so nearly did her heavy, compactly crouched figure, wound about with Eastern stuffs and glistening with gold, recall the images we are accustomed to associate with the worship of Vishnu. Her face, too, so far as it was visible in the subdued light, had the unresponsiveness of carven wood, and if not exactly hideous of feature, had in it a strange and haunting quality calculated to impress a sensitive mind with a sense of implacable fate. Cruel, hard, passionless, and yet threatening to a degree, must this countenance have seemed to those who willingly subjected themselves to its baneful influence.

I was determined not to be one of these, and yet I had not regarded her for two minutes before I found myself forgetting the real purpose of my visit, and taking a seat with the rest, in anticipation of something for which as yet I had no name, even in my own mind.

How long I sat there motionless I do not know. A spell was on me—a spell from which I suddenly roused with a start. Why or through what means I do not know. Nobody else had moved. Fearing a relapse into this trance-like state, I made a persistent effort to be freed from its dangers. Happily the full signification of my errand there burst upon me. Finding myself really awake, I ventured to peer about, expecting to see the more willing devotees affected as

I had been. I encountered a flash from the eyes of the young lady whose bag I held in my hand. She was under no spell. She had not only seen but recognized me.

I held the bag towards her. She gave a furtive glance in the direction of Madame—a glance not free from fear—then clutched the bag. Before releasing my hold upon it I ventured upon a word of explanation. I got no further, for at this moment a voice was heard.

By the effect it had upon the expectant ones, I knew it could have emanated only from the idol-like being who had filled the place with her awesome personality.

At first the voice sounded like a distant call, musically sweet and low; the kind of note that we can imagine the Indian snake-charmers to use when the cobra raises its winged head in obedience to the pipe's resistless charm. Every ear was strained to hear; mine with the rest. So much preparation, so much faith must result in something. What was it to be? The incoherent sounds became more and more distinct, and, finally, took on the articulate form of words. The quiet was deathly. Every one was prepared to interpret her utterances into personal significance. The dread and trouble of the times filling all minds, men wished to be forehanded with the decrees of Providence. Into this brooding silence the low, vibrating tones of this mysterious voice entered, and this is what we heard:

"Doom! doom! For him—the one—the betrayer—the passing bell is tolling. Hear it, ye weak ones and grow strong. Hear it, ye mighty and tremble. Not alone for him will it ring. For ye! for ye! if the decree of the linked rings goes forth—-"

Here there was a perceptible quiver of the drapery back of the dais. Others may not have noted it; I did. When, therefore, a very white hand came slowly from between its folds and placed its fingers upon the right temple of Madame, I was not much startled. What did startle me was the fact let out before that admonishing hand touched her, that this being—I can hardly call her woman—seemingly so far removed from the political agitations of the day, was, in very deed, either consciously or unconsciously—I could not decide which—intimately connected with the conspiracy I was at that very moment striving to defeat. How intimately? Was she the prime mover I was seeking, or simply an instrument under the control of another, and yet stronger, personality imaged in the owner of that white hand?

There was no means of determining at that moment. Meanwhile, the fingers had left the temple of Madame. The hand was slowly withdrawn. Sleep apparently fell again upon the dreamer, but only long enough for her to bring forth the words:

"I have said."

The silence that followed, gave me time to think. It was necessary. She had bidden the mighty tremble and had pronounced death to one—the betrayer. Was this senseless drivel, prophetic sight, or threatened murder? I inclined to consider it the last, and this was why: For some weeks now, murder, or, at least, sudden death, had been rampant in the country. My flesh crept as I remembered the many mysterious deaths reported within the month from St. Louis, Boston, New Orleans, New York and even here in Baltimore. Like a flash it came across me that every name was identified, more or less closely, with the political affairs of the time. Coupling my knowledge with what I conjectured, was it strange I saw a confirmation of the worst fears expressed by Miss Calhoun in the half-completed sentences of this seeming clairvoyant?

So occupied had I been with my own thoughts that I feared I might have done something to call an undesirable attention to myself. Glancing furtively to one side, I heard, in the opposite direction, these words:

"She has never failed. What she has said will come to pass. Some one of note will die."

These gloomy words were the first to break the ominous silence. Turning to face the speaker, I encountered the cold eye of a man with a retreating chin, a receding forehead, and a mouth large and cruel enough to stamp him as one of those perverted natures who, to the unscrupulous, are usefully insane.

Here, then, was a being who not only knew the meaning of the fateful words we had heard, but, to my mind, could be relied upon to make them a verity.

It was a relief to me to turn my gaze from his repellant features to the fixed countenance of Madame. She had not stirred; but either the room had grown lighter or my eyes had become more accustomed to the darkness, for I certainly saw a change in her look. Her eyelids were now raised, and her eyes were bent directly upon me. This was uncomfortable, especially as there was malevolence in her glance, or so I thought, and, far from being pleased with my position, I began to wish that I had never allowed myself to enter the place. Under the influence of this feeling I let my eyes drop from the woman's countenance to her hands, which were folded, as I have said, in a fixed position across her breast. The result was an increase of my mental disturbance. They were brown, shining hands, laden with rings, and, in the added light, under which I saw them, bore a strange resemblance to the bronze hand I had just left in Dr. Merriam's office.

I had never considered myself a weak man, but, from that instant, I began to have a crawling fear of this woman—a fear that was in nowise lessened by the very evident agitation visible in the girl, who had been for me the connecting link between that object of mystery and this.

Unendurable quiet was upon us all again. It was aggravated by awe—an awe to which I was determined not to succumb, notwithstanding the secret uneasiness under which I was laboring. So I let my eyes continue to roam, till they fell upon the one thing moving in the room. This was a man's foot, which I now saw projecting from behind the drapery through which I had seen the white hand glide. It was swinging up and down in an impatient way, so out of keeping with the emotions perceptible on this side of the drapery that I felt forced to ask myself what sort of person this could be who thus kept watch and ward with such very commonplace impatience over a creature who was able to hold every other person in her presence under a spell. The drapery did not give up its secrets, and again I yielded to the fascinations of Madame's face.

There was a change in it; the eyes no longer looked my way, but into space, which seemed to hold for them some terrible and heart-rend-ing vision. The lips, which had been closed, were now parted, and from them issued a breath which soon formed itself into words.

"'Vengeance is mine! I will repay,' saith the Lord." What passionate utterance was this? The voice that had been musical now rang with jangling discord. The swinging of the foot behind the drapery ceased. Madame spoke on:

"Through pain, sorrow, blood and death shall victory come. Life for life, pang for pang, scorn for scorn!"

The swinging foot disappeared, and the small white hand passed quickly through the curtain and rested again upon the forehead of Madame. But without a calming effect this time. On the contrary, it seemed to urge and incite her, for she broke into a new strain, speaking rapidly, wildly, as if she lived in what she saw, or, what was doubtless truer, had lived in it and was but recalling her own past in one of those terrible hours of memory that recur on the border-land of dreams.

"I see a child, a girl. She is young; she is beautiful. Men love her, many men, but she loves only one. He is of the North; she is of the South. He is icy like his clime; she is fiery like her skies. The fire cannot warm the ice. It is the ice puts out the fire! Woe! woe!"

The left hand came from the drapery; found its way to the left temple of the woman. But it, too, was ineffectual. Hurriedly, madly, the words went on, tripping each other up in their haste and passion. The voice now became hoarse with rage.

"The girl is now a woman. A child is given her. The man demands the child. She will not give it up. He curses it; he curses her, but she is firm and holds it to her breast till her arms are blackened by the blows he deals her. Then he curses her country, the land that gave her a heart; and, hearing this, she rises up and curses him and his with an oath the Lord will hear and answer from His judgment throne. For the child was slain between them and its pitiful, small body blocks the passage of Mercy between his and hers forever. Woe! woe!"

As suddenly as the vehement change had come upon her, she had become calm again. The eyes retained their stony stare, but a cold and cruel smile formed about her lips, as if, with the utterance of that last word, she saw a futurity of blood and carnage satisfying her ferocious soul.

It was revolting, horrible; but no one else seemed to feel it as I did. To most it was a short glimpse into a suffering soul. To me it was the revelation of causes which had led, and would lead yet, to miseries for which she had no pity, and which I felt myself too weak to avert.

That it was not intended that the devotees of Madame should have heard these ravings was evident; for at this juncture the owner of the two white hands that had failed to control the spirit of

Madame came out from behind the drapery of the dais. He proved to be none other than the man with the bristling mustache whose plans I had disarranged at the doctor's office by plugging the keyhole of the box with wax.

This was enough. "Chicanery!" was my inmost thought as I noted his cool and calculating eye. "But very dangerous chicanery," I added. Was the ring upon whose immediate capture I now saw that a life, if not lives, depended, in his possession, or in that of Madame, or in that of the Quaker-like girl sitting a few seats from me? How impossible to tell, and yet how imperative to know! As I was debating how this could be brought about, I watched the man.

Self-control was a habit with him, but I saw the nervous clutch of his delicate hand. This did not indicate complete mastery of himself at that moment. He spoke with care, but as if he were in haste to deliver himself of the few necessary words of dismissal, without betraying his lack of composure.

"Madame will awake presently; she will be heard no more to-day. Those who wish to kiss her robes may pass in front of her; but she is still too far away from earth to hear your voices or to answer any questions. You will therefore preserve silence."

So! so! more chicanery. Or was it strategy, pure and simple? Was there at the bottom of his words the wish to see me nearer or was he just playing with the credulity of such believers as the man next me, for instance? I did not stop to determine. My anxiety to see Madame, without the illusion of even the short distance between us, induced me to join the file of the faithful who were slowly approaching the seated woman. I would not kiss her robes, but I would look into her eyes and make sure that she was as far away from us all as she was said to be.

But as I drew nearer to her I forgot all about her eyes in the interest awakened by her hands. And when it came my turn to pause before her, it was upon the middle finger of her right hand my eyes were fixed. For there I saw THE RING; the veritable ring of my fair neighbor, if the description given by her was correct.

To see it there was to have it; or so I vowed in my surprise and self-confidence. Putting on an air of great dignity, I bowed to the woman and passed on, resolving upon the course I would pursue, which must necessarily be daring in order to succeed. At the door I paused till all who followed me had passed out; then I turned back, and once again faced Madame.

She was alone. Her watchful guardian had left her side, and to all appearances the room. The opportunity surpassed my expectations, and with a step full of nerve I pushed forward and took my stand again directly in front of her. She gave no token of seeing me; but I did not hesitate on that account. Exerting all my will power, I first subjected her to a long and masterful look, and then I spoke, directly and to the point, like one who felt himself her superior,

"Madame," said I, "the man you wish for is here. Give me the ring, and trust no more to weak or false emissaries."

The start with which she came to life, or to the evidence of life, was surprising. Lifting her great lids, she returned my gaze with one equally searching and powerful, and seeing with what disdain I sustained it, allowed an almost imperceptible tremor to pass across her face, which up to now had not displayed the shadow even of an emotion.

"You!" she murmured, in a dove-like tone of voice; "who are you that I should trust you more than the others?"

"I am he you expect," said I, venturing more as I felt her impassibility giving way before me. "Have you had no premonition of my coming? Did you not know that he who controls would be in your presence to-day?"

She trembled, and her fingers almost unclasped from her arms.

"I have had dreams," she murmured, "but I have been bidden to beware of dreams. If you are the person you claim to be, you will have some token which will absolve me from the charge of credulity. What is your token?"

Though doubtful, I dared not hesitate. "This," I said, taking from my pocket the key which had been given me by my fair neighbor.

She moved, she touched it with a finger; then she eyed me again.

"Others have keys," said she, "but they fail in the opening. How are you better than they?"

"You know," I declared—"you know that I can do what others have failed in. Give me the ring."

The force, the assurance with which I uttered this command moved her in spite of herself. She trembled, gave me one final, searching look, and slowly began to pull the ring from off her finger. It was in her hand, and half way to mine, when a third voice came to break the spell.

"Madame, Madame," it said; "be careful. This is the man who clogged the lock, and hindered my endeavors in your behalf in the doctor's office."

Her hand which was so near mine drew back; but I was too quick and too determined for her. I snatched the ring before she could replace it on her own hand, and, holding it firmly, faced the intruder with an air of very well-assumed disdain.

"Attempt no argument with me. It was because I saw your weakness and vulgar self-confidence that I interfered in a matter only to be undertaken by one upon whom all can rely. Now that I have the ring, the end is near. Madame, be wiser in the choice of your confidants, To-morrow this ring will be in its proper place."

Bowing as I had done before, I advanced to the door. They had made no effort to regain the ring, and I felt that my rashness had stood me in good stead. But as, with a secret elation I was just capable of keeping within bounds, I put my foot across the threshold, I heard behind me a laugh so triumphant and mocking that I felt struck with consternation; and, glancing down into my hand, I saw that I held, not the peculiar steel circlet destined for the piece of mechanism in the doctor's office, but an ordinary ring of gold.

She had offered me the wrong ring, and I had taken it, thus proving the falsity of my pretensions.

There was nothing left for me but to acknowledge defeat by an ignominious departure.

IV. CHECKMATE.

I HASTENED at once home, and knocked at Miss Calhoun's door. While waiting for a response, the mockery of my return without the token I had undertaken to restore to her, impressed itself upon me in full force. It seemed to me that in that instant my face must have taken on a haggard look. I could not summon up the necessary will to make it otherwise. Any effort in that direction would have made my failure at cheerfulness pitiable.

The door opened. There she stood. Whatever expectancy of success she may have had fled at once. Our eyes met and her countenance changed. My face must have told the whole story, for she exclaimed:

"You have failed!"

I was obliged to acknowledge it in a whisper, but hastened to assure her that the ring had not yet been placed upon the bronze hand, and was not likely to be till the lock had been cleaned, out. This interested her, and called out a hurried but complete recital of my adventure. She hung upon it breathlessly, and when I reached the point where Madame and her prophetic voice entered the tale, she showed so much excitement that any doubts I may have cherished as to the importance of the communication Madame had made us vanished in a cold horror I with difficulty hid from my companion. But the end agitated her more than the beginning, and when she heard that I had taken upon myself a direct connection with this mysterious matter, she grew so pale that I felt forced to inquire if the folly I had committed was likely to result badly, at which she shuddered and replied:

"You have brought death upon yourself. I see nothing but destruction before us both. This woman—this horrible woman—has seen your face, and, if she is what you describe, she will never forget it. The man, who is her guardian or agent, no doubt, must have tracked you, and finding you here with me, from whose hand he himself may have torn the ring last night, will record it as treason against a cause which punishes all treason with death.

"Pshaw!" I ejaculated, with a jocular effort at indifference, which I acknowledge I did not feel. "You seem to forget the law. We live in the city of Baltimore. Charlatans such as I have just left behind me do not make away with good citizens with impunity. We have only to seek the protection of the police."

She met my looks with a slowly increasing intentness, which stilled this protest on my lips.

"I am under no oath," she ruminated. "I can tell this man what I will. Mr. Abbott, there has been formed in this city an organization against which the police are powerless. I am an involuntary member of it, and I know its power. It has constrained me and it has constrained others, and no one who has opposed it once has lived to do so twice. Yet it has no recognized head (though there is a chief to whom we may address ourselves), and it has no oaths of secrecy. All is left to the discretion of its members, and to their fears. The object of this society is the breaking of the power of the North, and the means by which it works is death. I joined it under a stress of feeling I called patriotism, and I believed myself right till the sword was directed against my own breast. Then I quailed; then I began to ask by what right we poor mortals constitute ourselves into instruments of destruction to our kind, and having once stopped to question, I saw the whole matter in such a different light that I knowingly put a stumbling-block in the path of so-called avenging justice, and thus courted the doom that at any moment may fall upon my head." And she actually looked up, as if expecting to see it fall then and there. "This Madame," she went on in breathless haste, "is doubtless one of the members. How so grotesque and yet redoubtable an individuality should have become identified with a cause demanding the coolest judgment as well as the most acute political acumen, I cannot stop to conjecture. But that she is a member of our organization, and an important one, too, her prophecies, which have so strangely become facts, are sufficient proof, even had you not seen my ring on her finger. Perhaps, incredible as it may appear, she is the chief. If so— But I do not make myself intelligible," she continued, meeting my eyes. "I will be more explicit. One peculiar feature of this organization is the complete ignorance which we all have concerning our fellow-members. We can reveal nothing, for we know nothing. I know that I am allied to a cause which has for its end the destruction of all who oppose the supremacy of the South, but I cannot give you the name of another person attached to this organization, though I feel the pressure of their combined power upon every act of my life. You may be a member without my knowing it—a secret and fearful thought, which forms one of the greatest safeguards to the institution, though it has failed in this instance, owing"—here her voice fell—"to my devotion to the man I love. What?"—(I had not spoken; my heart was dying within me, but I had given no evidence of a wish to interrupt her; she, however, feared a check, and rushed vehemently on.) "I shall have to tell you more. When, through pamphlets and unsigned letters—dangerous communications, which have long since become ashes—I was drawn into this society (and only those of the most radical and impressionable natures are approached) a ring and a key were sent me with this injunction: 'When the man or woman whose name will be forwarded to you in an otherwise empty envelope, shall have, in your honest judgment, proved himself or herself sufficiently dangerous to the cause we love, to merit removal, you are to place this ring on the middle finger of the bronze hand locked up in the box openly displayed in the office of a Dr. Merriam on ——— Street. With the pressure of the whole five rings on the fingers of this piece of mechanism, the guardian of our rights will be notified by a bell, that a victim awaits justice, and the end to be accomplished will be begun. As there are five fingers, and each one of these must feel the pressure of its own ring before connection can be made between this hand and the bell mentioned, no injustice can be done and no really innocent person destroyed. For, when five totally disconnected persons devoted to the cause agree that a certain individual is worthy of death, mistake is impossible. You are now one of the five. Use the key and the ring according to your conscience.' This was well, if I had been allowed to follow my conscience; but when, six weeks ago, they sent me the name of a man of lofty character and unquestioned loyalty, I recoiled, scarcely believing my eyes. Yet, fearing that my own judgment was warped, or that some hidden hypocrisy was latent in a man thus given over to our attention, I made it my business to learn this man's inner life. I found it so beautiful——" She choked, turned away for a moment, controlled herself, and went on rapidly and with increased earnestness: "I learned to love this man, and as I learned to love him I grew more and more satisfied of the dangerous character of the organization I was pledged to. But I had one comfort. He could not be doomed without my ring, and that was safe on my finger. Safe! You know how safe it was. The monster whom you have just seen, and who may have been the person to subject this noble man to suspicion, must have discovered my love and the safeguard it offered to this man. The ring, as you know, was stolen, and as you have failed to recover it, and I to get any reply from the chief to whom I forwarded my protest, to-morrow will without doubt see it placed upon the finger of the bronze hand. The result you know. Fantastic as this may strike you, it is the dreadful truth."

Love, had I ever felt this holy passion for her, had no longer a place in my breast; but awe, terror and commiseration for her, for him, and also perhaps for myself, were still active passions within me, and at this decided statement of the case, I laughed in the excitement of the moment, and the relief I felt at knowing just what there was to dread in the adventure.

"Absurd!" I cried. "With Madame's address in my mind and the Baltimore police at my command, this man is as safe from assault as you or I are. Give me five minutes' talk with Chief——"

Her hand on my arm stopped me; the look in her eye made me dumb.

"What could you do without me?" she said; "and my evidence you cannot have. For what would give it weight can never pass my lips. The lives that have fallen with my connivance stand between me and confession. I do not wish to subject myself to the law."

This placed her in another light before me, and I started back.

"You have——" I stammered.

"Placed that ring three times on the hand in Dr. Merriam's office."

"And each time?"

"A man somewhere in this nation has died suddenly. I do not know by what means or by whose hand, but he died."

This beautiful creature guilty of—— I tried not to show my horror.

"It is, then, a question of choice between you and him?" said I. "Either you or he must perish. Both cannot be saved."

She recoiled, turning very pale, and for several minutes stood surveying me with a fixed gaze as if overcome by an idea which threw so immense a responsibility upon her. As she stood thus, I seemed not only to look into her nature, but her life. I saw the fanaticism that that had once held every good impulse in check, the mistaken devotion, the unreasoning hatred, and, underneath all, a spirit of truth and rectitude which brightened and brightened as I watched her, till it dominated every evil passion and made her next words come easily, and with a natural burst of conviction which showed the innate generosity of her soul.

"You have shown me my duty, sir. There can be no question as to where the choice should fall, I am not worth one hair of his noble head. Save him, sir; I will help you by every means in my power."

Seizing the opportunity she thus gave me, I asked her the name of the man who was threatened.

In a low voice she told me.

I was astonished; dumfounded.

"Shameful!" I cried. "What motive, what reason can they have for denouncing him?"

"He is under suspicion—that is enough."

"Great heaven!" I exclaimed. "Have we reached such a pass as that?"

"Don't," she uttered, hoarsely; "don't reason; don't talk; act."

"I will," I cried, and rushed from the room.

She fell back in a chair, almost fainting. I saw her lying quiet, inert and helpless as I rushed by her door on my way to the street, but I did not stop to aid her. I knew she would not suffer it.

The police are practical, and my tale was an odd one. I found it hard, therefore, to impress them with its importance, especially as in trying to save Miss Calhoun I was necessarily more or less incoherent. I did succeed, however, in awakening interest at last, and, a man being assigned me, I led the way to Madame's door. But here a surprise awaited me. The doorplate, which had so attracted my attention, was gone, and in a few minutes we found that she had departed also, leaving no trace behind her.

This looked ominous, and with little delay we hastened to the office of Dr. Merriam. Knocking at the usual door brought no response, but when we tried the further one, by which his patients usually passed out, we found ourselves confronted by the gentleman we sought.

His face was calm and smiling, and though he made haste to tell us that we had come out of hours, he politely asked us in and inquired what he could do for us.

Not understanding how he could have forgotten me so soon, I looked at him inquiringly, at which his face lighted up, and he apologetically said:

"I remember you now. You were here this morning consulting me about a friend who is afflicted with a peculiar complaint. Have you anything further to state or ask in regard to it. I have just five minutes to spare."

"Hear this gentleman first," said I, pointing to the officer who accompanied me.

The doctor calmly bowed, and waited with the greatest self-possession for him to state his case.

The officer did so abruptly.

"There is a box in your ante-room which I feel it my duty to examine. I am Detective Hopkins, of the city police."

The doctor, with a gentleness which seemed native rather than assumed, quietly replied:

"I am very sorry, but you are an hour too late." And, throwing open the door of communication between the two rooms, he pointed to the table.

The box was gone!

V. DOCTOR MERRIAM.

This second disappointment was more than I could endure. Turning upon the doctor with undisguised passion, I hotly asked:

"Who has taken it? Describe the person at once. Tell what you know about the box, I did not finish the threat; but my looks must have been very fierce, for he edged off a bit, and cast a curious glance at the officer before he answered:

"You have, then, no ailing friend? Well, well; I expended some very good advice upon you. But you paid me, and so we are even."

"The box!" I urged; "the box! Don't waste words, for a man's life is at stake."

His surprise was marvelously assumed or very real.

"You are talking somewhat wildly, are you not?" he ventured, with a bland air. "A man's life? I cannot believe that."

"But you don't answer me," I urged.

He smiled; he evidently thought me out of my mind.

"That's true; but there is so little I can tell you. I do not know what was in the box about which you express so much concern, and

I do not know the names of its owners. It was brought here some six months ago and placed in the spot where you saw it this morning, upon conditions that were satisfactory to me, and not at all troublesome to my patients, whose convenience I was bound to consult. It has remained there till to-day, when——"

Here the officer interrupted him.

"What were these conditions? The matter calls for frankness."

"The conditions," repeated the doctor, in no wise abashed, "were these: That it should occupy the large table in the window as long as they saw fit. That, though placed in my room, it should be regarded as the property of the society which owned it, and, consequently, free to the inspection of its members but to no one else. That I should know these members by their ability to open the box, and that so long as these persons confined their visits to my usual hours for patients, they were to be subject to no one's curiosity, nor allowed to suffer from any one's interference. In return for these slight concessions, I was to receive five dollars for every day I allowed it to stay here, payment to be made by mail."

"Good business! And you cannot tell the names of the persons with whom you entered into this contract?"

"No; the one who came to me first and saw to the placing of the box and all that, was a short, sturdy fellow, with a common face but very brilliant eye; he it was who made the conditions; but the man who came to get it, and who paid me twenty dollars for opening my office door at an unusual hour, was a more gentlemanly man, with a thick, brown mustache and resolute look. He was accompanied——"

"Why do you stop?"

The doctor smiled.

"I was wondering," said he, "if I should say he was accompanied, or that he accompanied, a woman, of such enormous size that the doorway hardly received her. I thought she was a patient at first, for, large as she is, she was brought into my room in a chair, which it took four men to carry. But she only came about the box."

"Madame!" I muttered; and being made still more eager by this discovery of her direct participation in its carrying off, I asked if she touched the box or whether it was taken away unopened.

The doctor's answer put an end to every remaining hope I may have cherished.

"She not only touched but opened it. I saw the lid rise and heard a whirr. What is the matter, sir?"

"Nothing," I made haste to say—"that is, nothing I can communicate just now. This woman must be followed," I signified to the officer, and was about to rush from the room when my eye fell on the table where the box stood.

"See!" said I, pointing to a fine wire protruding from a small hole in the center of its upper surface; "this box had connection with some point outside of this room."

The doctor's face flushed, and for the first time he looked a trifle foolish.

"So I perceive now," said he, "The workman who put up this box evidently took liberties in my absence. For that I was not paid."

"This wire leads where?" asked the officer.

"Rip up the floor and see. I know no other way to find out."

"But that would take time, and we have not a minute to lose," said I, and was disappearing for the second time when I again stopped. "Doctor," said I, "when you consented to harbor this box under such peculiar conditions and allowed yourself to receive such good pay for a service involving so little inconvenience to yourself, you must have had some idea of the uses to which so mysterious an article would be put. What did you suppose them to be?"

"To tell you the truth, I thought it was some new-fangled lottery scheme, and I have still to learn that I was mistaken."

I gave him a look, but did not stop to undeceive him.

VI. THE BOX AGAIN.

But one resource was left: to warn Mr. S—— of his peril. This was not so easy a task as might appear. To make my story believed, I should be obliged to compromise Miss Calhoun, and Mr. S———'s well-known chivalry, as far as women are concerned, would make the communication difficult on my part, if not absolutely impossible. I, however, determined to attempt it, though I could not but wish I were an older man, with public repute to back me.

Though there was but little in Mr. S———'s public life which I did not know, I had little or no knowledge of his domestic relations beyond the fact that he was a widower with one child. I did not even know where he lived. But inquiry at police headquarters soon settled that, and in half an hour after leaving the doctor's office I was at his home.

It was a large, old-fashioned dwelling, of comfortable aspect; too comfortable, I thought, for the shadow of doom, which, in my eyes, overlay its cheerful front, wide-open doors and windows. How should I tell my story here! What credence could I expect for a tale so gruesome, within walls warmed by so much sunshine and joy. None, possibly; but my story must be told for all that.

Ringing the bell hurriedly, I asked for Mr. S———. He was out of town. This was my first check. When would he be home? The answer gave me some hope, though it seemed to increase my difficulties. He would be in the city by eight, as he had invited a large number of guests to his house for the evening. Beyond this, I could learn nothing.

Returning immediately to Miss Calhoun, I told her what had occurred, and tried to impress upon her the necessity I felt of seeing Mr. S——— that night. She surveyed me like a woman in a dream. Twice did I have to repeat my words before she seemed to take them in; then she turned hurriedly, and going to a little desk standing in one corner of the room, drew out a missive, which she brought me. It was an invitation to this very reception which she had received a week before.

"I will get you one," she whispered. "But don't speak to him, don't tell him without giving me some warning. I will not be far from you. I think I will have strength for this final hour."

"God grant that your sacrifice may bear fruit," I said, and left her.

To enter, on such an errand as mine, a brilliantly illuminated house odoriferous with flowers and palpitating with life and music, would be hard for any man. It was hard for me. But in the excitement of the occasion, aggravated as it was by a presage of danger not only to myself but to the woman I had come so near loving, I experienced a calmness, such as is felt in the presence of all mortal conflicts. I made sure that this was reflected in my face before leaving the dressing-room, and satisfied that I would not draw the attention of others by too much or too little color, I descended to the drawing-room and into the presence of my admired host.

I had expected to confront a handsome man, but not of the exact type that he presented. There was a melancholy in his expression I had not foreseen, mingled with an attraction from which I could not escape after my first hurried glimpse of his features across the wide room. No other man in the room had it to so great a degree, nor was there any other who made so determined an effort to throw off care and be simply the agreeable companion. Could it be that any other warning had forestalled mine, or was this his habitual manner and expression? Finding no answer to this question, I limited myself to the duty of the hour, and advancing as rapidly as possible through the ever-increasing throng, waited for the chance to speak to him for one minute alone. Meantime, I satisfied myself that the two detectives sent from police headquarters were on hand. I recognized them among a group of people at the door.

Whether intentionally or not, Mr. S——— had taken up his stand before the conservatory, and as in my endeavors to reach him I approached within sight of this place, I perceived the face of Miss Calhoun shining from amid its greenery, and at once remembered the promise I had made her. She was looking for me, and, meeting my eyes, made me an imperceptible gesture, to which I felt bound to respond.

Slipping from the group with which I was advancing, I stole around to a side door towards which she had pointed, and in another moment found myself at her side. She was clothed in velvet, which gave to her cheek and brow the colorlessness of marble.

"He is not as ignorant of his position as we thought," said she. "I have been watching him for an hour. He is in anticipation of something. This will make our task easier."

"You have said nothing," I suggested.

"No, no; how could I?"

"Perhaps the detectives I saw there have told him."

"Perhaps; but they cannot know the whole."

"No, or our words would be unnecessary."

"Mr. Abbott," said she, with feverish volubility, "do not try to tell him yet; wait for a few minutes till I have gained a little self-possession, a little command over myself; but no—that may be to risk his life—do not wait a moment—go now, go now, only——" She started, stumbled and fell back into a low seat under a spreading palm. "He is coming here. Do not leave me, Mr. Abbott; step back there behind those plants. I cannot trust myself to face him all alone."

I did as she bade me. Mr. S——, with a smile on his face—the first I had seen there—came in and walked with a quick step and a resolved air up to Miss Calhoun, who endeavored to rise to meet him. But she was unable, which involuntary sign of confusion seemed to please him.

"Irene," said he, in a tone that made me start and wish I had not been so amenable to her wishes, "I thought I saw you glide in here, and my guests being now all arrived, I have ventured to steal away for a moment, just to satisfy the craving which has been torturing me for the last hour. Irene, you are pale; you tremble like an aspen. Have I frightened you by my words—too abrupt, perhaps, considering the reserve that has always been between us until now. Didn't you know that I loved you? that for the last month—ever since I have known you, indeed—I have had but the one wish, to make you my wife?"

"Good God!" I saw the words on her lips rather than heard them. She seemed to be illumined and overwhelmed at once. "Mr. S———," said she, trying to be brave, trying to address him with some sort of self-possession,

"I did not expect—I had no right to expect this honor from you. I am not worthy—I have no right to hear such words from your lips. Besides——" She could go no further; perhaps he did not let her.

"Not worthy—you!" There was infinite sadness in his tone. "What do you think I am, then? It is because you are so worthy, so much better than I am or can ever be, that I want you for my wife. I long for the companionship of a pure mind, a pure hand——"

"Mr. S———" (she had risen, and the resolve in her face made her beauty shine out transcendently), "I have not the pure mind, the pure hand you ascribe to me. I have meddled with matters few women could even conceive of. I am a member—a repentant member, to be sure—of an organization which slights the decrees of

God and places the aims of a few selfish souls above the rights of man, and——"

He had stooped and was kissing her hand.

"You need not go on," he whispered; "I quite understand. But you will be my wife?"

Aghast, white as the driven snow, she watched him with dilating eyes that slowly filled with a great horror.

"Understand!—you understand! Oh, what does that mean? Why should you understand?"

"Because"—his voice sunk to a whisper, but I heard it, as I would have recognized his thought had he not spoken at that moment—"because I am the chief of the organization you mention. Irene, now you have my secret."

I do not think she uttered a sound, but I heard the dying cry of her soul in her very silence. He may have heard it, too, for his look showed sudden and unfathomable pity.

"This is a blow to you," he said. "I do not wonder; there is something hateful in the fact; latterly I have begun to realize it. That is why I have allowed myself to love. I wanted some relief from my thoughts. Alas! I did not know that a full knowledge of your noble soul would only emphasize them. But this is no talk for a ballroom. Cheer up, darling, and——"

"Wait!" She had found strength to lay her hand on his arm. "Did you know that a man was condemned to-day?"

His face took on a shade of gloom.

"Yes," he bowed, casting an anxious look towards the room from which came the mingled sounds of dance and merriment. "The bell which announces the fact rang during my absence. I did not know there was a name before the society."

She crouched, covering her face with her hands. I think she was afraid her emotion would escape her in a cry. But in an instant they had dropped again, and she was panting in his ear:

"You are the chief and are not acquainted with these matters of life and death? Traitors are these men and women to you—traitors! jealous of your influence and your power!"

He looked amazed; he measured the distance between himself and the door and turned to ask her what she meant, but she did not give him the opportunity.

"Do you know," she asked, "the name of the person for whom the bell rang to-day?"

He shook his head. "I am expecting a messenger with it any moment," said he, looking towards the rear of the conservatory. "Is it any one who is here to-night?"

The gasp she gave might have been heard in the other room. Language and motion seemed both to fail her, and I thought I should have to go to her rescue. But before I could move, I heard the click of a latch at the rear of the conservatory, and saw, peering through the flowers and plants, the wicked face of the man with the receding forehead whom I had seen at madame's, and in his arms he held THE BOX.

It was a shock which sent me further into concealment. Mr. S——, on the contrary, looked relieved. Exclaiming, "Ah, he has come!" he went to the door leading into the drawing-room, locked it, took out the key and returned to meet the stealthy, advancing figure.

The latter presented a picture of malignant joy, horrible to contemplate. The lips of his large mouth were compressed and bloodless. He came on with the quiet certainty and deadly ease of a slimy thing sure of its prey.

As I noted him I felt that not only Mr. S——'s life but my own was not worth a moment's purchase. But I uttered no cry and scarcely breathed. Miss Calhoun, on the contrary, gave vent to a long, shivering sigh. The man bowed as he heard it, but with looks directed solely to Mr. S——.

"I was told," said he, "to deliver this box to you wherever and with whomsoever I should find you. In it you will find the name."

Mr. S—— gazed in haughty astonishment, first at the box and then at the man.

"This is irregular," said he. "Why was I not made acquainted with the fact that a name was up for consideration, and why have you removed the box from its place and broken the connection which was made with so much difficulty?"

As he said this he looked up through the glass of the conservatory to a high building I could see towering at the end of the garden. It was the building in which I had first seen that box, and I now understood how this connection had been made.

Mr. S——'s movement had been involuntary.

Dropping his eyes, he finished by saying, with an almost imperceptible bow, "You may speak before this lady; she is the holder of a key."

"The connection was broken because suspicion was aroused; to your other question you will find an answer in the box. Shall I open it for you?"

Mr. S———, with a stern frown, shook his head, and produced a key from his pocket. "Do you understand all this?" he suddenly asked Miss Calhoun.

For reply, she pointed to the box.

"Open!" her beseeching looks seemed to say.

Mr. S——— turned the key and threw up the lid. "Look under the hand," suggested the man.

Mr. S——— leaned over the box, which had been laid on a small table, discovered a paper somewhere in its depth, and drew it out. It was no whiter than his face when he did so.

"How many have subscribed to this?" he asked.

"You will observe that there are five rings on the hand," responded the man.

Miss Calhoun started, opened her lips, but paused as she saw Mr. S——— unfold the paper.

"The name of the latest traitor," murmured the man, with a look of ferocity the like of which I had never seen on any human face before.

It was not observed by either of the actors in the tragedy before me. Mr. S——— was gazing with a wild incredulity at the note he had unfolded; she was gazing at him. From the room beyond rose and swelled the sweet strains of the waltz.

Suddenly a low, crackling sound was heard.

It came from the paper which Mr. S——— had crumpled in his hand.

"So the society has decreed my death," he said, meeting the man's steel-cold eye for the first time. "Now I know how the men whose doom preceded mine have felt in a presence that leaves no hope to mortal man. But you shall not be my executioner. I will meet my fate at less noxious hands than yours." And, leaning forward, he whispered a few seemingly significant words into the messenger's ear. The man, grievously disappointed, hung his head, and with a sidelong look, the venom of which made us all shudder, he hesitated to go.

"To-night?" he said.

"To-night," Mr. S—— repeated, and pointed towards the door by which he had entered. Then, as the man still hesitated, he took him by the arm and resolutely led him through the conservatory, crying in his ear, "Go. I am still the chief."

The man bowed, and slipped slowly out into the night.

A burst of music, laughter, voices, joy, rose in the drawing-room. Mr. S—— and Irene Calhoun stood looking at each other.

"You must go home," were the first words he uttered. Then, in a half-reproachful, half-pitiful tone, as if on the verge of tears, he added: "Was I so bad a chief that even you thought me a hindrance to the advancement of the society and the cause to which we are pledged?"

It was the one thing he could say capable of rousing her.

"Oh!" she cried, "it is all a mistake, all a cheat. Did you not get the letter I sent to my chief this morning, written in the usual style and directed in the usual way?"

"No," he answered.

"Then there is worse treason than yours among the five. I wrote to say that my ring had been stolen; that I did not subscribe to the condemnation of the man under suspicion, and that, if it was made, it would be through fraud. That was before I knew that the suspected one and the man I addressed were one and the same. Now——"

"Well, now?"

"You have but to accuse the woman called Madame. The man you have just sent away would forgive you his disappointment if you gave him the supreme satisfaction of carrying doom to the still more formidable being who prophesies death to those for whom she has already prepared a violent end."

"Irene!"

But her passion had found vent and she was not to be stilled. Telling him the whole story of the last twenty-four hours, she waited for the look of comfort she evidently expected. But it did not come. His first words showed why.

"Madame is inexorable," said he; "but Madame is but one of five. There are three others—true men, sound men, thinking men. If they deem me unworthy—and I have shown signs of faltering of late—Madame's animosity or your loving weakness must not stand in the way of their decree. It shall never be said I sanctioned the doom of other men and shrank from my own. I would be unworthy of your love if I did, and your love is everything to me now." She had not expected this; she had not at all reckoned upon the stern quality in this man, forgetting that without it he could never have held his pitiless position.

"But it is not regular; it is not according to precedent. Five rings are required, and only four were fairly placed. As an honest man, you ought to hesitate at injustice, and injustice you will show if you allow them to triumph through their own deceit."

But even this failed to move him.

"I see five rings," said he, "and I see another thing. Never will I be permitted to live even if I am coward enough to take advantage of the loophole of escape you offer me. A man who is once seen to tremble loses the confidence of such men as call me chief. I would die suddenly, horribly and perhaps when less prepared for it than now. And you, my darling, my imperial one! you would not escape. Besides, you have forgotten the young man who, with such unselfishness, has lent himself to your schemes in my favor. What could save him if I disappointed the malignancy of Madame. No; I have destroyed others, and must submit to the penalty incurred by murder. Kiss me, Irene, and go. I command it as your chief."

With a low moan she gave up the struggle. Lifting her forehead to his embrace, she bestowed upon him a look of indescribable despair, then tottered to the door leading into the garden. As it closed upon her departing figure, he uttered a deep sigh, in which he seemed to give up life and the world. Then he raised his head, and in an instant was in the midst of a throng of beautiful women and dashing men, with a smile on his lips and a jest on his tongue.

I made my escape unnoticed. The next morning I was in Philadelphia. There I read the following lines in the leading daily:

"Baltimore, Md.—An unexpected tragedy occurred here last evening. Mr. S——, the well-known financier and politician, died at his supper-table, while drinking the health of a hundred assembled guests. He is considered to be a great loss to the Southern cause. The city is filled with mourning."

And further down, in an obscure corner, this short line:

"Baltimore, Md.—A beautiful young woman, known by the name of Irene Calhoun, was found dead in her bed this morning, from the effects of poison administered by herself. No cause is ascribed for the act."

Made in United States
North Haven, CT
07 September 2022